S0-AHG-322

Every Dog Has His Day

John R. Erickson

Illustrations by Gerald L. Holmes

Puffin Books

To the members of the
Texas Library Association

PUFFIN BOOKS
Published by the Penguin Group
Penguin Putnam Books for Young Readers,
345 Hudson Street, New York, New York 10014, U.S.A.
Penguin Books Ltd,
27 Wrights Lane, London W8 5TZ, England
Penguin Books Australia Ltd,
Ringwood, Victoria, Australia
Penguin Books Canada Ltd,
10 Alcorn Avenue, Toronto, Ontario, Canada M4V 3B2
Penguin Books (N.Z.) Ltd,
182-190 Wairau Road, Auckland 10, New Zealand

Penguin Books Ltd, Registered Offices:
Harmondsworth, Middlesex, England

First published in the United States of America by
Maverick Books, Gulf Publishing Company, 1988
Published by Puffin Books, a member of
Penguin Putnam Books for Young Readers, 1999

1 3 5 7 9 10 8 6 4 2

LIBRARY OF CONGRESS CATALOGING-IN-PUBLICATION DATA
Erickson, John R.
Every dog has his day / John Erickson ; illustrations by Gerald L. Holmes.
p. cm.
Originally published in series: Hank the Cowdog ; 10.
Summary: Hank the Cowdog gets into more trouble before he is able
to find a happy solution to his problems.
ISBN 0-14-130386-7 (pbk.)
[1. Dogs—Fiction. 2. West (U.S.)—Fiction. 3. Humorous stories.] I. Holmes,
Gerald L., ill. II. Title. III. Series: Erickson, John R. Hank the Cowdog ; 10.
PZ7.E72556Ev 1999 [Fic]—dc21 98-41808 CIP AC

Printed in the United States of America

CONTENTS

CHAPTER ONE

The Case of
the Jingling Bells

It's me again, Hank the Cowdog. When you've been on the side of law and order as long as I have, it's hard to get used to being a fugitive and an outcast.

But that's by George what happened in June of whatever year that was when it happened—last year, I suppose you might say. But it definitely happened.

I'll take first things first and one thing at a time because I've found, over my years in security work, that it just doesn't pay to do it any other way. This job pays little enough under the best of circumstances, and how did I get on the subject of pay?

It's an important subject but it seems to me

that I had something else on my mind. I'll get it here in a minute. Weather's been nice, hasn't it? Had a little shower the other morning.

What the heck was I going to talk about? It really burns me up when I . . . oh yes. The fugitive and outcast business.

Okay, here we go. This may turn out to be one of my more exciting stories, so hang on. It started out as a normal day in June. I had been out on routine patrol most of the night, checking things out, making sure my ranch was secure from coyotes, coons, skunks, badgers, and the many species of monsters we have around here.

At daylight, everything checked out, so I went down to the sewer and freshened up and made my way to the gas tanks, where I had every intention of keeping a date with my gunnysack bed.

Drover was there, as you might have guessed, wheezing and twitching in his bed. He heard me pawing at my gunnysack and opened one eye. His eyeball went around in circles.

"You should have someone look at that eye, Drover. There's something wrong with it."

"Tblckw dkvlskc with murgle skiffer."

"Maybe so, but that doesn't alter the fact that it goes around in circles. And speaking of circles, did you make your patrol? I'll need a full report on conditions in the eastern quadrant of head-quarters. Might as well get it over with now, before I go off duty."

"Lorken tonsils skiffer murgle skungling pork chops."

"How can you be sure of that? Did you check it out yourself or is it just hearsay?"

"Humlum morkin reskiffering sardines."

"And you're positive about that?"

His other eye slid open and he stared at me for a moment. "Where am I?"

"That depends on your location, Drover. Once you get that settled, the rest of it will fall into place. Where were you the last time you remembered?"

"I don't remember."

I flopped down on my gunnysack and released my grip on the world. "That's one of your problems, son. You need to work on developing your memory. Memory is very crucial to success in the security business. Try it again, and this time, concentrate."

"Okay. What am I concentrating on?"

"You're concentrating on trying to remember."

"Oh. Remembering what?"

"Remembering where you were the last time you were somewhere."

"Boy, that's a tough one."

"Yes, but I don't need to remind you that you

3

could use a little toughening up. Go ahead and scuffle with it. When you come up with an answer, wake me up."

"You going to sleep?"

"Not entirely. Although it may appear that I'm falllllling azzzzzzleep, tblckw dkvlskc with murgle skiffer."

"Oh good. It sure gets boring around here when I have to think and remember. Now let's see, where was I the last time I was somewhere?"

"Lorken tonsils skiffer murgle skungling pork chops."

"No, I don't think so, because that would have made it Saturday and that was the day all the clouds went over, wasn't it? Clouds sure are pretty."

"Humlum morkin reskiffering sardines."

"Sometimes I wish I could be a cloud. Wouldn't that be fun, just float around all day and take naps and skiffer murgle chicken bone."

"Mumlumnum hoosh."

"Lumnum hooshy morkin skumble."

"Zzzzzzzzzzzz."

"Zzzzzzzzzz."

I must admit that some of this conversation didn't make sense to me, for you see, Drover fell asleep. Another thing that didn't make sense was that, suddenly, I heard the jingling of distant bells.

My ears shot up and I leaped to my feet. "Zzzwait a minute, pork chops don't sound like that! Wake up, Drover, I think I've got it."

His eyelids popped open, revealing two crossed eyes behind them. "Clouds ride chicken bone motorcycles. What?"

"I said, wake up, I think I've got it. It's all coming clear now. If the bells are jingling, this must be Christmas!"

He staggered to his feet and walked around in a circle. "Oh my gosh, do they bite?"

"What?"

"Where am I?"

"How should I know where you are, and what difference does it make? The point is that there's something very strange going on here and it's our job to sound the alarm, so don't just bark there. Stand!"

"Oh, okay." The little dunce just stood there.

"Are you going to bark or not?"

"You said to stand here. I think that's what you said."

"It's time for you to stop thinking, Drover, and trust your cowdog instincts, even though you're not a cowdog. There's a time to stand up for what you believe in and there's a time to think, but this is the time to bark your little heart out."

"Oh, okay."

"Because something very strange is going on around here."

He rolled his eyes around. "What is it?"

"I . . . I don't remember what it is, but that's neither here nor there. Bark, Drover, that's the important thing right now!"

And that's just what we did. We gave whatever it was a good old-fashioned barking, I with my deep masculine roar and Drover adding his yip-yip-yip. We must have barked for a solid minute, and at the end of that time my head had begun to clear.

"Wait a minute, hold on, Drover. What are we barking at?"

"I don't know. I asked you that a while ago, and you said . . ."

"Never mind what I said. It's foolish for us to waste our reserves if we don't know what we're barking at. Let me think." I thought. "Yes, it's coming back to me now. I heard bells, Drover, the jingling of bells. And I guess you know what that means."

"No, I don't think I do."

"Good, because I don't either, but that's the whole point. If we heard bells jingling and can't

6

define the source, then what we have here is the Case of the Jingling Bells."

"Oh my gosh!"

"Yes indeed. Now listen very carefully." He was staring up at the sky. "Are you listening very carefully?"

"What? No, I was just looking at the clouds. There sure are a lot of clouds this morning."

"Never mind the clouds. Pay attention. In thirty seconds, we will proceed to Checkpoint Charlie. I'll go first. You guard the flanks and the rear. We're going to find out who or whom has been jingling those alleged bells, and I don't need to tell you that this could get us into some combat. You ready?"

"I guess."

"All right. Form a line, pick up your feet, and let's move out."

We went streaking toward the saddle shed, the point from which the jingling bells had come from. I took the lead and Drover brought up the rear.

By this time it had become clear to me that both Drover and I had fallen asleep beneath the gas tanks and that this probe of the enemy's position had grown out of a fairly incoherent conversation.

Nevertheless, it had to be checked out. Sometimes your best leads in this business come from strange sources. A good cowdog will check them all out. It's just part of the job.

We went crashing through some tall weeds, and by the time we reached a point adjacent to the point at which the garden lay adjacent to the saddle shed, I heard the bells again. And this time I couldn't dismiss it as a mere dream or a product of Drover's shriveled intelligence.

Yes indeed, we had bells on the ranch. I hadn't cleared anyone to jingle bells on my ranch, and I was fixing to pull rank and give somebody a rude surprise.

"All right, Drover," I yelled over my shoulder, "let's initiate Barking Mode One. Ready? BARK!"

Fellers, we barked! Maybe I don't need to point out how difficult it is to go into Barking Mode One while running at top speed, but it's a pretty nifty trick that requires concentration and a good deal of raw athletic ability.

When I saw the saddle shed door hanging open, I knew we had ourselves a live one. Something or someone had broken in there—without clearance, I might add—and we had caught the culprits in an unauthorized entry. As you might have guessed, I don't allow unauthorized entries on my outfit.

In other words, they had made a very serious miscalculation and had walked right into my trap. For you see, there was only one door into the saddle shed, which meant there was only one door OUT. We had them cornered.

"All right, Drover, we'll take up positions in front of the door and initiate Barking Mode Two. When they come out, give them the full load. I'll go for the first one, you take the second one."

"What if there's three?"

"If there's three, Drover, we'll play it by ear. Ready? Bark!"

We sent up an amazing barrage of barking, just by George fractured the silence of morning with alarms and threatening sounds. Even though we had the situation pretty well under control, it wouldn't have made me mad if High Loper had come rushing down from the house with his gun.

Well, we were in the midst of our barking procedure when all of a sudden a two-legged, human-type monster leaped out the door. He had two clawed hands and a ferocious expression on his face. Oh yes, and he made a terrible sound: "HEE-YAHHHH!"

The hair shot up on the back of my neck and my deep roar of a bark suddenly turned into a squeak, and you might say that I plowed little Drover under trying to get away from the monster, thought I would give a little ground, see, and then establish another . . .

Let me say here that the cowboys on this outfit have a twisted sense of humor, and sometimes I get the feeling that they don't take my job as seriously . . .

Okay, maybe it was Slim. Maybe the jingling bells had actually been his spurs. Maybe he was trying to be funny, jumping out the door with his claws out. But the point is that nobody had cleared . . . never mind.

CHAPTER TWO

A Working Hippopotamus Takes Shape

Oh, he got a big chuckle out of it, Slim did, just laughed and howled and held his sides and fell on the ground. I didn't think it was so funny myself.

"Did you think I was going to get you, Hankie? You'd better be more careful what you bark at." He went back into the saddle shed, chuckling to himself. It's always a little shocking to realize how childish these cowboys can be.

Well, it took me a whole minute to get the hair to lay back down on my neck, and then I looked around for Drover. He had disappeared. I went looking for him, figgered he might have

11

high-balled it up to the machine shed, but I found him hiding behind one of them big Chinese elms just east of the garden. I could see his eyes peeking around the trunk.

"You can come out now, Drover."

"What was that thing?"

"Just Slim, trying to be funny."

"Oh. Sure didn't look like Slim to me."

"First impressions are often wrong, Drover. You must learn to probe deeper and look for the forest instead of the trees."

Drover stared at me and twisted his head. "I thought you said it was Slim."

"I did say it was Slim."

"Oh. I thought that's what you said, but then you said he was a tree."

"No, you weren't paying attention. How could Slim be a tree?"

"I don't know. I didn't think he looked much like a tree. He didn't have enough bark."

"He didn't bark at all, Drover. WE barked at HIM."

"Yeah, I know, but he didn't have enough bark to be a tree."

"Of course he didn't, you dunce, because trees don't bark! Now stop wasting my time and . . ." All at once I heard a pickup coming down the road from the mailbox. "Wait a minute, what is this?"

Drover looked up. "I think it's a tree."

"What? No, coming down the road."

"Oh. Gosh, it looks like a pickup to me."

"Indeed it is a pickup, pulling a green stock trailer. The question is, what is it doing on my ranch?"

"Beats me, but I wonder what it's doing here?"

"Good question, Drover, and we're fixing to find some answers. Come on!"

We went streaking toward the unidentified pickup and barked it all the way down to the corrals. Just as I was about to sniff out the tires and mark them for future reference, another pickup came rolling in. And another!

I called to Drover and we went rushing out to meet the trespassers, gave each one of them as much of a barking as we could manage under the circumstances. Something very strange was going on here, and I needed to find out what it was.

I picked up some clues right away. All three of the pickups were pulling stock trailers. All three stock trailers had four wheels. Two were green and one was brown—no pattern there, but I noticed it anyway. And finally, inside each of the trailers was a horse—not the same horse, you see, but three different horses—and all three horses were saddled.

The drivers got out and two of them stretched their arms. I recognized two out of the three suspects. One was named Baxter, the other was Billy. Both lived on ranches down the creek, which meant they were neighbors. I didn't recognize the third man.

Oh, and they were all wearing spurs and chaps. That was kind of revealing too. When the neighbors come prowling around in shurs and spaps, spurs and chaps, that is, it usually indicates that some type of work is planned for the day.

I called my assistant over for a conference. "Drover, circulate around, sniff things out, keep your ears open. Something's going on around here."

"I thought so."

I glared at the runt. "Maybe you thought so, but I thought so first. Don't forget who's in charge around here."

"Oh, okay."

"Now get going. I'll expect a full report."

"Okay, Hankie, here I go!" And off he went.

I had my doubts that he would turn up any good leads, but when you're short-handed, you have to use whatever warm bodies happen to be

15

available. Drover was what you would call your Basic Warm Body.

I slipped around the pickups and trailers and checked things out, marked a few tires, kept my eyes and ears open, continued gathering data and amassing clues. When High Loper came down from the house, wearing his summer leggins and big-rowel spurs, I had enough evidence to come up with a Working Hypothenus . . .

Hypotenuse. Hypodermicus. Hyrolysis. What is the dadgummed word? Hippopotamus.

. . . I had turned up enough evidence to form a Working Hippopotamus: Without consulting me, the cowboys had decided to roundup and brand one of the pastures. Furthermore, they had invited strangers to come onto the ranch to help, with the work—again, without consulting me.

Well, this discovery really burned me up. I mean, running a ranch is hard enough under the best of circumstances, but when your own people start slipping around and making plans behind your back, it's really tough. But never mind, that's just part of the job.

I was in the process of sniffing tires and sifting clues when I heard a voice coming from the pickup above me: "Well, hello there, big boy. Imagine meeting you here!"

I froze. Hadn't I heard that sultry voice before? Hadn't I experienced that sudden increase in heart rate and blood pressure that I now felt? The answer was yes, I had, and it had been caused by a certain gorgeous beagle dog named Miss Scamper.

I lifted my eyes and saw her head protruding over the side of the pickup bed. Description: lovely brown eyes with big lashes, long beagle ears, a freckled nose, a very exciting pair of jowls.

Even though my deepest heart of hearts belonged to my one and only true love, Miss Beulah the Collie . . . MERCY! Furthermore, the last time Beulah and I had met, she had snubbed me for a worthless, stick-tailed, spotted bird dog named Plato, and I hadn't forgotten that snub or quite forgiven her for choosing a bird dog over a cowdog, and . . . MERCY!

"Well, blow me down," I said, "I believe I've just stumbled upon one of the seven wonders of the world."

"You could be right, but I didn't know there were six others."

"I may have miscounted, Miss Scamper. What's a nice place like you doing in a dog like this?"

"I just came along for the ride, thought I might, ah, see some different scenery."

"Well, I don't know how the scenery looks to

you, ma'am, but from down here, it's just pretty awesome."

"This must be your lucky day."

"Indeed it is, Miss Scamper, which brings to mind a poem:

Roses are red, the gas tanks are gray
Holy tamales, it's my lucky day!"

She winked. "Not bad, for a big old hunk of dog like you."

"Would you like to hear another one?"

"Oooo! I'm not sure I can stand it, but let's give it a try."

"All right. Hang on, here we go:

Roses are red but your face is incredible
I'd gobble you up if I thought you were
     edible."

She rolled her eyes. "I'm so impressed with your poetry!"

"Hey, that's only the beginning. Can you stand another one?"

"Just one more. I'll try not to faint."

"Fair enough. Here we go:

Roses will readily stab you with thorns
But this ache in my heart ain't caused by a
    rosebush."

The smile faded from her lips. "I think you missed on that one, big boy. It didn't exactly rhyme."

"Well, no, but that was a modern poem. They're not supposed to rhyme."

"I see. You just have an answer to every little question, don't you?"

"Yes ma'am. I not only have answers to every little question, but I have answers to several big ones. Furthermore, I have answers to questions that haven't even been asked yet."

"How interesting!"

"And speaking of questions, what do you have planned for the next thirty years?"

I gave her a wink and she gave me one back. "I'll, ah, have to look at my calendar and . . . ooooo, what have we here!"

Her eyes seemed to be looking past me. I turned my head and found myself peering into the face of a dog I had never seen before, didn't know, and didn't particularly want to know.

Description: black and white, long hair, long nose, medium height and build, pretty good conformation. In some ways, he resembled your border collie, a breed of dogs known for their ability to herd sheep.

On closer inspection, I began to suspect that he not only bore some faint resemblance to the border collie, but that he was a border collie, possibly one with papers and hot-rod breeding.

How could I have known all that in such a short span of time? Good question. The answer lies in my remarkable powers of concentration and a certain sixth sense I have about bloodlines. I mean, I can just by George look at a dog and pretty muchly tell you where he came from.

This one not only had the markings of a low-class sheepdog, but he also grinned all the time. Always grinning, that's the border collie. It comes from the fact that they go around with their mouths open and their tongues hanging off to one side. (Try that yourself and see if it doesn't make you grin.)

Let me pause here to point out that I've never had much use for dogs that fool with sheep, nor have I ever trusted a dog that went around grinning all the time, and furthermore, I didn't care for the way Miss Scamper was making eyes at this one.

I had a feeling that me and this sheep-herder weren't going to become bosom pals any time soon.

CHAPTER THREE

Benny
the Cowdog

I glared at the stranger and he grinned back at me. Then he spoke. "Good morning, sport, perfect day for a roundup, wouldn't you say?"

"I don't know as I'd say that at all. I've only seen a small part of this day and..."

He wasn't listening. "And what have we here?" He looked up at Miss Scamper with glittering eyes. "My, my! I don't think we've met, have we?"

Miss Scamper fluttered her eyelashes. "Not yet, but I have a feeling that could change at any moment."

"Indeed it could, you're very perceptive, Miss..."

"Scamper."

"Miss Scamper! What a lovely name, my goodness, there's poetry in it and music, and my goodness, aren't you a pretty little thing!"

"That's what I've heard," she said in her sultry voice, "and from some ver-ry reliable sources. And what might your name be, if I might be so brazen as to ask?"

"Benny the Cowdog, my good lady."

"Don't jump to any hasty conclusions about the 'good lady' business, and I'm so, SO happy to meet you."

"My goodness." The mutt turned to me and winked, as though we were best of friends, which we weren't. "This one could turn out to be a real bombshell. Are you her father?"

"No."

"She's a doll, pops. You ought to be proud of her."

"I am proud of her."

"That's what I like to hear, a father who's proud of his girl. That's really touching, pops, that's okay."

I moved closer and gave him a withering glare. "My name isn't Pops. I'm not her father. You're butting into my conversation, and you're on my ranch."

"Huh? Are you the yard dog or what?"

"I'm Hank the Cowdog, Head of Ranch Security." For the first time, he stopped grinning.

He stared at me and then burst out laughing. "Did I say something funny?"

He looked up at Miss Scamper. "Did he say he was a cowdog?" She nodded, and he turned back to me. "Did you say cowdog or *plowdog*?"

"I said cowdog, and that's what I meant. And before you get into any more trouble, I'll need to check your identification."

"Identification, yes, we have that, we sure do. Shall I start with my sire and dam? Both grand champions. Grandfather swept the Ft. Worth show four years in a row. Mom and Dad practically owned the Abilene stock dog trials, I mean, it was almost embarrassing. And my brothers..."

"That's probably enough," I said. "What you're trying to tell us is that you're pretty hot stuff."

"I'm not sure I would have put it in those exact words, but...yes. When you consider the breeding, the training, the contests, the winnings—well, most dogs find it overwhelming and more than a little intimidating."

"That so?"

"Yes, we've found that to be the case most of the time." He cast a leering eye at Miss Scamper. "What do you say, Sweetness?"

"Ah, well, I think I'm about to be overwhelmed and intimidated."

Benny turned back to me and shrugged. "We see this all the time."

"Well, it's a shame you can't stay longer."

"Oh, I am going to stay longer. I'm here for a demonstration with the cattle. I'm told it could turn into a permanent job."

"It could turn into a permanent injury. I take care of the cattle work on this outfit."

He was still grinning. "I don't know quite how to put this, but apparently someone thinks this ranch needs a good stock dog."

I moved a step closer. My patience was wearing thin. "Apparently someone was wrong. Get back in your pickup and wait for further orders."

"Sorry, old sport, but I take my orders from higher authorities."

There's a time for talk and there's a time for action. It was time to teach this dog a few lessons about higher authorities. I bristled up and made a dive at him. You might say that I missed.

"You're a little clumsy with that move, sport. I could give you a few pointers on your technique."

I made another dive at him and missed again. He was quicker than you might have thought.

"You're about half a step behind, it seems to me."

We glared at each other. Or put it this way: I

glared at him and he grinned at me, while I tried to think of something clever to say that might explain why I had missed him twice in a row. But just then, Drover came rushing up.

"Hank, I found out what's going on! It's round-up day, they're having a roundup right here on the ranch, and that's why all these pickups pulled in!"

"Very good, Drover. Did you figure that out yourself?"

"Yes! Well, no, I heard Slim talking about it, and did you know there's a famous dog here too? He's a champion cowdog and he's won contests and everything and . . ." It was then that Drover saw the stranger. "Oh my gosh, I bet that's him!"

Benny grinned and dipped his head. "I've been discovered, it seems."

Drover began groveling and turning in circles. "I've never met a famous dog before, boy, this is so exciting, I just don't know what to say!"

I glared at the runt. "Drover, when you have nothing to say, one of your alternatives is to keep your trap shut. That way, nobody will ever know how little they missed."

"I know, that's what I ought to do, but he's famous and . . . oh my gosh!" It was then that Drover saw Miss Scamper, and that finished him off. He rolled over on his back and started kicking his legs in the air.

Benny walked over for a closer look. "It seems the little fellow's had an attack of some sort."

"Get up, Drover, you're making a spectacle of yourself, and what's more important, you're making ME look bad."

"I'd say so, yes," said Benny, giving his head a shake, "it gives a bad impression of the ranch."

Drover opened his eyes and blinked them.

"Where am I?"

"Just where you were before you made a fool of yourself."

"Hank, will you deliver an important message for me?"

"What message, and to who or whom?"

"Tell Miss Scamper that I think I love her."

Miss Scamper heard the message and arched one brow. "My goodness, that's three in a row! This could turn out to be one of my better days."

"Get up, Drover, and stop talking nonsense. This is roundup day and we've got work to do."

"Well, not really," Benny butted in. "I'll be in charge of the roundup and I doubt that I'll need any help."

I turned away from Drover and gave our uninvited guest some fangs. "Let's get something straight, pardner. My ranch, my roundup. If you want to tag along and see how we do things on this outfit, okay. But keep your opinions to yourself."

I was all set to clean house on that guy once and for all. I mean, patience is a virtue only up to a point, and then it's time to start busting heads.

But just then, I heard High Loper call my name. I turned to Mister Smarty and gave him a smirk. "There, you see whose name they're call-

ing? You'll find that when the chips are down, they're very seldom up, and good management calls in the First String."

"Really? We'll see, I suppose."

"I suppose we will, and we'll just see whose cow ate the cabbage."

"I don't follow that."

"It's just as well that you don't, because you're going to stay right here while I go up and get my orders for this roundup. Drover, on your feet and prepare to move out. I'll be right back with our assignments."

The little mutt staggered to his feet. "Maybe I'd better stay here and guard Miss Scamper's pickup, 'cause my leg . . ."

"Never mind your leg. It's your so-called brain that I'm worried about. Don't say anything stupid until I get back."

"Oh. Okay."

And with that, I gave Miss Scamper one last wink, whirled around, and marched straight to the corrals, where the High Command was waiting to begin the strategy conference.

They couldn't start without me.

CHAPTER FOUR

HUH?

The cowboys were gathered around the door of the saddle shed. Loper was crouched down, doodling in the dust with his finger, which seemed a little odd to me.

I marched right into the center of things, which is sort of where you would expect the Head of Ranch Security to go, right? I sat down and waited for the conference to begin.

Loper's head came up. "You're sitting on my map of the pasture, you idiot."

I glanced around the circle of faces, searching for the alleged "idiot" who had . . .

"WILL YOU MOVE YOUR WORTHLESS CARCASS!"

He appeared to be looking at . . . well, ME, you

might say. I gave him a smile and began sweeping the ground with my tail.

"GET OFF MY MAP!"

I looked around for this map he was yelling about, and I'll be derned if I could see one. Obviously, he was speaking to someone else, yet he continued to glare at me and yell. So I, not knowing anything better to do, acted on a sudden impulse and licked him on the face.

Maybe that was the wrong sudden impulse to act upon. I mean, let's examine the facts: some guys appreciate a juicy lick on the face and some don't; sometimes it's just the right way to start off the morning and sometimes it ain't. At a high level conference, you just never know.

The point I'm sort of easing into is that Loper grabbed me and threw me out of the inner circle, while the others laughed and slapped their knees, and then he went back to drawing in the dust with his finger.

Oh. He was making a map of the . . . how was I supposed to know? He re-drew the pasture in the dust. I poked my head in between several pairs of legs and observed.

"Slim, you and Baxter take this trail up the caprock and check out the northwest corner. If you find any cattle, push them east toward me. I'll be

over in the northeast corner. We'll push everything south and try to bunch them in the prairie dog flat northeast of the house. You got that?"

The men nodded. So did I.

"All right, Billy, you cross the creek and ride out the south side. I noticed a big bunch over in the southeast corner yesterday evening."

Billy nodded. So did I. It was a pretty simple strategy, really, the same one I would have suggested.

"Johnny, you take the dog and ride down the creek to the Parnell water gap. There's a bunch of tamaracks and willows down there, and that's where the dog might make a hand. Turn him loose in that brush and see if he can bring the cattle out."

Johnny nodded. So did I. Loper was exactly right in thinking that I could bring those cattle out of the heavy brush. That's one of my specialties, brush work.

You'll find that some of your modern-day, lower-bred stock dogs won't do brush work. For example, you hear a lot of these blue heelers nowadays complaining about thick brush. They don't like it. They'd rather sit in the back of a pickup in front of the coffee shop and growl at everyone who goes in and out.

I never had much use for the coffee shop crowd myself, and heavy brush has never bothered me in the least. As far as I'm concerned, the heavier the brush, the thicker it is, and I like to be in the thick of things. So there you are.

It struck me as a little odd that Loper had assigned me to work with Johnny, a man I didn't know. A lot of dogs would find it difficult, if not impossible, to coordinate complex pasture maneuvers and command systems with a total stranger.

Me? I take things as they come. Loyalty to the outfit is very high on my list, and if that means working with a stranger—hey, I'll be there, covering my territory and doing my job.

"Any questions?" Nobody had a question. Loper pushed himself up to a standing position and I noted that his knees popped. I salted that information away for future reference. You never know when mere information might turn into a valuable clue.

"Boys," Loper went on, "I'll be riding a green colt this morning. If the cattle make a run, you boys with better horses will have to go with the leaders and I'll stay with the drag." They nodded. "Baxter, will that beagle dog of yours stay in the pickup?"

"Oh yeah, she's trained, and she don't have much use for cattle anyway. She'll stay in the pickup."

"Good. That leaves us with just one worthless dog to worry about."

Ho ho! Benny was fixing to get himself tied up or locked up or otherwise removed from the roundup strategy. It couldn't have happened to a nicer dog or come at a better time.

I had tried to prepare him for this, but some dogs just can't seem to take a hint.

"Come on, Hank."

This was turning out even better than I had hoped! I would get to watch the scoundrel take his medicine. I could hardly wait to see that grin melt off his mouth.

I fell in step beside Loper and we went marching . . . that was odd. Instead of marching toward Benny, we headed east, toward the house. Oh well. Loper had his own way of handling the "worthless dog" situation, as he had described it so well, and I had every confidence that . . .

We marched up the hill, past the roping dummy, past the gas tanks, up to the yard gate. Just as I had predicted, he bent over and picked up a piece of rope, some ten feet in length, that was tied to the gate post.

I sat down and looked back toward the pickups, waiting for Loper to call the unsuspecting
Benny up for his, shall we say, "roundup assignment." Heh heh. I could hardly conceal my...

HUH?

Unless I was badly mistaken, Loper had
just...wait a minute, there must be some...he
hadn't even called Benny and...hey, he had tied
up the wrong dog!

I looked up at him, gave him my most wounded look, and whapped my tail on the ground. He cupped his hands around his mouth and called Drover. In a flash the runt was there, grinning, turning in circles, and wagging his stump tail.

Loper jammed his hands on his hips. "You dogs stay out of the way and keep quiet. We're going to see a REAL dog in action today, and I don't want you to mess up his work. You got that?"

By this time, Drover was in the middle of one of his guilt spasms, when he rolls around on the ground and kicks his legs in the air and pulls his lips up into a simple-looking grin and seems to be apologizing for every mistake that's been made since the beginning of time.

I don't know why he does that. If you ask me, it's undignified.

Anyway, Loper stomped back down to the corral, leaving me tied up and psychologically damaged.

"Gee, you got tied up, didn't you, Hank?"

"Wipe that silly grin off your face."

"Oh, okay." The silly grin vanished and was replaced by Drover's patented blank expression. "You got tied up, didn't you?"

"It may appear that way at first glance, Drover, but on second glance . . . yes. Of course, I

don't need to tell you that someone on this ranch has just made an enormous mistake."

"Oh, you didn't need to tell me that."

"I know I didn't, which is why I said so, but I thought I'd say it anyway."

"I thought that's what you thought that's what you'd say, and I'm glad you said it anyway."

"Well, I'm glad you're glad."

"I thought you would be."

"Do you have any idea what you're saying?"

"No, what?"

"Absolutely nothing. You're just spouting nonsense."

"Well, you keep answering me."

"Answers are not the question, Drover."

"No, I guess not."

"And questions are not the answer."

"It gets kind of confusing, doesn't it?"

"And while we're on the subject of questions, I have one for you."

"Oh good, and I have one for you too."

"I'll go first, since mine is the more important of the two."

"Oh, I don't know. Mine's pretty important."

"I doubt that, but just to prove what a wonderful dog I am, I'll let you go first."

"Gee thanks, Hank. That's mighty nice of you."

"Yes, I know. Go ahead." I waited, while Drover squinted his eyes and twisted his mouth around. "You'll have to speak a little louder, son, I can't hear you."

"I didn't say anything."

"I know you didn't say anything. That's my whole point. Hurry up and ask your question, I have important things to do."

"What can you do when you're tied up?"

"ASK YOUR QUESTION!"

"Oh. Well, let's see here. It was right on the tip of my tongue, and it sure was important. You don't remember what it was, do you?"

"Of course I don't. How could I remember something I never knew in the first place?"

"I don't know, but I thought I'd check."

"Is it possible, Drover, that after I was generous enough to let you go first, you forgot your question?"

"Well . . . I didn't want to say that, 'cause it might have made you mad."

"Indeed it might have. Go ahead and admit it."

"I'd rather not, if it's all the same to you."

"It's not all the same to me. It's completely different, a brand new category of stupidity. Did you forget your question?"

"That's one way of putting it."

"In other words, yes, you did in fact forget your question."

"Something like that."

"Very well, that just proves what I've suspected for a long time: courtesy is wasted on you. In the future, I'll save my generosity for somebody who deserves it."

"Sorry, Hank, I tried."

"Never mind that you tried, Drover. The point is that you failed. And I guess you realize that this leaves me with no choice but to proceed to MY question."

"I guess so."

But you know what? After going through all that nonsense with Drover, I couldn't remember what I was going to ask him. That really burned me up, and it just goes to prove that . . . never mind.

Steel Cable Is
Hard to Chew

I've always loved spring roundup days—the clean smell of the air, the jingle of spurs, the laughter of the cowboys, the nickering of horses, the way the country looks when the sun pops up over the horizon and makes the dew glitter like diamonds.

And me down at the corrals, sharing the excitement with the cowboys and barking orders and taking charge of things and singing the "Saddle Up Overture in C-Maybe."

It's a real crackerjack of a song and I do it particularly well. The tune ain't all that great but I like the words. Here's how it goes:

Saddle Up Overture in C-Maybe

Saddle up, saddle up, saddle up, saddle up,
Saddle up, saddle up, saddle up, saddle up,
Saddle up, saddle up, saddle up, saddle up,
Saddle up, saddle up, saddle saddle up!

Saddle up, saddle up, saddle up, saddle up,
Saddle up, saddle up, saddle up, saddle up,
Saddle up, saddle up, saddle up, saddle up,

Saddle up, saddle up, saddle saddle up!

Saddle . . . etc.

Anyway, where was I? Oh yes, sitting by the yard gate, tied up like a common mutt and watching another dog take my place on the crew. Let me tell you, fellers, it almost broke my heart.

The cowboys mounted up and rode out across that grassy flat just south of the corrals. They were talking and laughing and playing with their ropes. Loper's colt was feeling frisky and started bucking. Loper put a good ride on him and the others cheered.

If I had been there with them, I would have barked, but of course I wasn't and so I didn't.

Benny the Imposter was there in my place, trotting along beside his master. I had to look away.

"Drover, this is a dark day in my life."

He rolled his eyes around. "Yeah, but it's getting brighter, now that the sun's up. The sun always seems to make the day brighter."

"I've been taken off the job, removed, replaced, cast aside like an old shoe. Nobody wants an old shoe, Drover."

"Yeah, they wear boots most of the time."

"Of course there is another alternative."

"You bet. They could go barefoot if it weren't for all the sticker weeds."

"Just because they've put me on a stake doesn't mean I have to swallow it."

"Heck no, but steak sure beats dog food."

"Anything that's been roped can be unroped. Anything that's tethered can be untethered. For you see, Drover, no knot is permanent."

"And if you know not, you're just plain ignert."

"Exactly. It seems that our minds are moving in the same direction, which is the true meaning of teamwork. I guess you've already figured out what our next move will be."

"Sure have. We'll just sit here and wait for Sally May to bring out the steak. Boy, I'm ready for one."

I stared at him. "What?"

"I said, boy, I'm ready for one."

"One *what*?"

"Steak."

"Steak?"

"Mistake?"

"You're ready for Sally May to bring out a mistake? What are you talking about, Drover?"

"I'm not sure. There for a minute I thought I had it, but I guess it slipped away."

"I guess it did. Are you ready to get me out of this rope?"

"Rope?"

I went nose-to-nose with the runt. "Yes, rope. That's what we've been talking about. Untie the knot and I'll get on with my business."

"Oh, okay." He spent two minutes gnawing at the knot and also my throat.

"Just the knot, Drover. Don't untie the throat."

"I don't think I can do it, Hank."

"All right, then chew the rope in half."

"Oh. You mean, just bite it?"

"That's correct. Pick it up in your teeth, bite it, chew it in half, and I'll be free."

"Well . . ." He took two little bites at the rope. "It tastes bad, Hank, and it hurts my teeth."

"Never mind how it tastes, and never mind about your teeth. Get on with the job!"

He started backing away. "To tell you the truth, I sort of wanted to go down and talk to Miss Scamper. I think she called my name."

I had taken just about all of Drover's insubordination that I could stand. I had given him a direct order and he had dared to talk back to me, which is something I don't tolerate. I roared, bared my fangs, and made a lunge at . . .

HUH?

All at once, I was lying on my back, looking up at the sky. I noticed an odd sensation in my neck, almost as though it had been stretched several inches.

Hmm, yes, the clues began falling into place. Post, rope, neck. You see, in making my lunge at Drover, I had reached the end of my tether. The tremendous force generated by my forward momentum . . .

In other words, Drover had escaped a thrashing by the narrowest of margins. Another couple of inches and I would have had him. At first glance, a couple of inches doesn't seem like much, but in the security business . . .

I picked myself off the ground and rolled a kink out of my neck. "Get your little self over here and do what you were told. Immediately!"

"Oh, I think I'll go talk to Miss Scamper, if it's all right with you."

"It's NOT all right with me. I forbid you to talk to Miss Scamper, and when I forbid something, that means it's forbidden."

"I know, Hank, but every now and then I feel a terrible weakness to do something forbidden."

"We call that a 'weakness,' Drover, and you must resist it."

He kept backing away. "I'm trying to resist it, but something keeps pulling me in that direction."

"It's your legs, Drover. Stop moving your legs and you'll become stationary."

"Can't do it, Hank. My legs keep moving."

"Drover, I forbid you to do anything forbidden."

"Help! I'm being pulled toward Miss Scamper!"

"I can't help you, I'm tied up!"

"I know you are, but I'm not. Bye." And with that, he went prancing down the hill.

It was all coming clear now. The puzzes of the piecle were falling into place, the pieces of the puzzle. Using his tiny brain as a defense against reality, Drover had surmised that, just because I was tied to the gate post, I couldn't stop him from going down to talk with Miss Scamper.

And furthermore, he was correct, which just goes to prove that a small brain is better than none at all, but in sizing up the situation, he had made one small miscalculation. For you see, he had overlooked the simple fact that I could chew my own rope in half. You might even say that, in the heat of the argument, I had overlooked this fact myself.

The point is, all I had to do was chew the rope in half. And that is precisely what I set out to do.

The fact that Drover had failed in this maneuver meant nothing to me, for what he lacked in intelligence, he also lacked in sharp teeth, jaw strength, and endurance.

I began the procedure by loosening up the enormous muscles in my jaws. I took the rope into my mouth, opened my jaws to their fully extended position, and CRUNCH! And then CRUNCH again. And one more CRUNCH! And then . . .

The derned rope did have a bad taste. It was a grass rope, don't you see, and it had been dipped in some kind of oil, and I never did care for the taste of oil, with the possible exception of bacon grease and chicken fat, but this stuff left a lousy taste in my mouth and . . .

There must have been something about that oil treatment that made the rope stouter than you might have thought, because what I'm driving at is that it remained more or less intact.

Come to think of it, that might have been half-inch steel cable instead of a grass rope.

Yes, it was.

So there I was, tied to a huge post with half-inch steel cable. My roundup had been taken over by an outsider and my assistant Head of Ranch Security was down under the trees, talking and giggling with Miss Scamper. And the whole thing left a bad taste in my mouth.

I didn't think the situation could deteriorate any more—until Pete the Barncat came along. And at that point, it deteriorated further.

(It really was steel cable.)

Using Laser
Logic on the Cat

I don't like Pete, never have. He's a perfect example of your sniveling, scheming, basically selfish and untrustworthy kind of cat. Like most cats, he's not too bright, yet he has a genius for showing up where he's not wanted.

Where he's not wanted is anywhere I happen to be, because, at the risk of repeating myself, I don't like him.

I saw him coming down the hill from the machine shed. He had his tail stuck straight up in the air. He was purring like a little chainsaw and rubbing up against shrubs and posts and everything else that couldn't kick him away.

Well, my ears shot up and my lips began to curl. Funny, how that happens. All I have to do is see that cat and these processes begin to take hold. I mean, it's completely automatic. The ears fly up and the lips rise, unsheathing a set of deadly fangs.

And did I mention the growl? Yes, a deep roar of a growl began to rumble in my lower throat—again, completely automatic.

"Stop right there, cat. You're approaching the Injury Zone. A few more steps and you'll be in the Zone of Sudden Death."

"Hi, Hankie. What you doing?"

"I'm minding my own business, which is something you ought to try sometime."

He smiled. "Nice day for a roundup, isn't it?"

"Maybe it is and maybe it ain't. Either way, it's nothing you need to worry about."

"I'm surprised you're not out gathering cattle."

"Oh yeah? Well, this life is full of surprises, and you're fixing to buy yourself a truckload of them."

He yawned and arched his back. "I like your new necktie, Hankie. You look good in that color."

"I look good in *any* color."

"Yes, but yellow just seems to fit you somehow."

"What do you mean by that? Explain yourself and be quick about it. If you mean what I think you mean, you've set a new record for getting yourself into serious trouble."

"Not a thing, Hankie. Just remember:

Sticks and stones may break your bones
But words will never hurt you."

"Oh yeah? Well, here's one for you:

Sticks and stones may break your bones
But I will break your neck.

"How do you like that one?"

"It's a little crude, but then," he grinned, "so are you."

"That's right, and proud of it."

He sat down in front of me, and the end of his tail began to twitch like a snake. "How long's your rope, Hankie?"

I was about to give him a stinging reply when, suddenly, I realized what he was doing. This cat was trying to lure me into an argument. What he didn't realize was that I had been trained for this sort of thing.

See, to get certified in security work, a guy has to go through a rigorous training period, where the emphasis is on self-discipline. The basic idea is simple. *When you're confronted by a taunting cat, you must realize what the cat is trying to do.*

That's the first step. Once you've figgered out

Step One, then you move on to Step Two.

In the Step Two Phase, you activate the iron discipline for which cowdogs are famous. We have certain exercises to strengthen our self-discipline, but I'm not at liberty to reveal them at this time, so we'll move along to Step Three.

In the Step Three Phase, we engage a powerful force called Laser Logic. Stripped of the complex technical termination, Laser Logic can be described as the secret weapon dogs use against cats and other obnoxious animals. It enables us to make very sophisticated plans, see, and to stay one step ahead of the enemy.

Do we have time for one quick example? Okay, take our present situation. This cat was trying to lure me into a fight. Your ordinary ranch dog would fall for this trick, in which case he would make a dive for the cat and merely prove what the cat had known all along, that the dog was tied up and therefore couldn't satisfy his desire to pulverize the stupid cat.

Your higher-bred, highly trained cowdog, on the other hand, will engage his Laser Logic and come up with a winning strategy. Instead of falling for the cat's trick, he turns the tables on the cat and DOES THE OPPOSITE OF EVERYTHING HE SAYS.

Amazing. Now watch and I'll demonstrate.

Okay, we've got Pete sitting there in front of me, twitching his stupid tail, which is something that really annoys me. And he says, "How long's your rope, Hankie?"

At that point, I engage Step One and move rapidly through Stage Two and into Stage Three, accomplish the whole thing in just a matter of seconds. And instead of losing my temper, barking, lunging against the rope, and so forth, I give him a friendly smile.

Now, listen to this.

"Why, I don't know how long it is, Pete, nor do I understand why you should care. But if you're really concerned about it, I'd be happy for you to measure it."

That's iron discipline right there.

"No, but I bet you could reach my tail if you really wanted to."

I studied his alleged tail, which he continued to twitch. "You're exactly right, Pete. I could, but I really don't have any interest in your tail."

Oh, that almost destroyed him! Laser Logic.

He moved a little closer and his tail drew some figure-eights in the air. "I'm sure you could reach it here."

I laughed. It's very satisfying to reach a level

of maturity at which you can laugh off all the silliness in this old world.

"You're right, Pete. Back in the old days, I would have made a dive for it, but I've developed other interests and I just don't have time for you or your childish games."

Stunned him, absolutely stunned him!

He moved a little closer. Hmm. He was getting within range now, and that tail . . . but iron discipline prevailed. Good old iron discipline.

"I'll bet you can't reach me here."

"HUH? What was that? Did you say I CAN'T reach you there?"

He bobbed his head up and down. "That's what I said, Hankie. I bet you can't."

For a moment there, I was confused. Pete had tabed the turnles on me, or you might say "turned the tables." Either way, the point is that he had shifted, in a typical sneaky catlike manner, the fulcrum of his attack.

That ploy might have worked, had I not been trained for this sort of thing. I was confused, but only for a few seconds. Then Laser Logic kicked in: DO THE OPPOSITE OF EVERYTHING HE SAYS. Before, he had said, "I bet you can reach my tail." Now, he was saying, "I bet you *can't* etc."

Indeed, he had shifted his strategy.

At that point, when most dogs would have gone into a period of confused barking, the Laser Logic System took over and I shifted into Automatic. My mind began gliding through the complex calculations.

The advantage of using higher mathematics and Laser Logic is that you avoid impulsive behavior and dumb mistakes. Also, once Laser Logic has solved the equation, a guy isn't burdened down by

$$(C1 - C2/2) \times 2.5(C1+C2) = ?$$

a bunch of unnecessary thinking. You just by George take your answer and get after it.

Which is exactly what I did. It was Double Sic 'Em time. I made a dive for the cat, with every intention of dividing his tail by two and multiplying that times deadly force.

He escaped by the narrowest of margins. He hissed, arched his back, raised the hair along his spine, flattened his ears, and backed away.

Hey, that didn't scare me, not even a little bit. In fact, that hissing stuff gets on my nerves and makes me even meaner, wilder, and ferociouser than ever.

I coiled my powerful legs under me and lunged at him and . . . GULK!

Hit the end of the derned rope, you might say, I'd sort of forgotten about that in the heat of, that might have been one factor we had forgotten to put into the . . .

Let me say this. It's hard to keep up a deep, thunderous bark when you have a tight rope against your throat, sort of throttles the thunder down to a squeak, and while a squeak is only a squeak, it beats the heck out of cowardly silence.

I barked. I squeaked. I lunged against the rope, tore up the ground, raised a cloud of dust, and snapped my jaws like a bear trap.

Obviously out-maneuvered, out-barked, and outsmarted, Pete took up a position just beyond my reach and ... well, popped me on the nose with his claws, you might say, every time I moved into his range, which was fairly often.

Yes, we lost a little blood and sustained a few casualties, but we expect that in an armed confrontation ...

Okay, it hurt. Let's go ahead and put that into the record. The nose did in fact take some direct hits, and there for a minute or two, it appeared that Pete was getting the better end of the deal.

But then something happened that changed everything. It came as a complete surprise to

Pete, but as you might have already guessed, it was no surprise to me, for it was merely Phase Two of my two-phase strategy.

Just as I had predicted, the rope broke. And suddenly, Pete's advantage turned to mush, as I not only snatched victory out of the jaws of defeat, but also snatched Pete into the Jaws of Destruction.

CHAPTER SEVEN

Miss Scamper
Is Impressed

You ever notice that once a cat finds himself in an awkward position, he begins scratching with all four sets of claws, front and back? He does.

Once this mechanism is invoked, a normal, healthy cat begins to resemble a buzz saw. You ever bite into a buzz saw? In the Security Business, we try to follow strict dietary laws: no sugar, very little salt, a bare minimum of cholestrophobia, and no buzz saws.

Buzz saws can cause bleeding gums and eyebrow damage.

In other words, anyone with an ounce of prevention would spit out a pound of buzz saw, which is basically what I did, because of my interest in diet and health.

Diet is extremely . . .

So you might say that Pete escaped my clutches and went streaking down the hill, past the gas tanks, through the grove of elm trees, and toward the corrals. I, dragging the rope, fell in behind him, bulldozed a couple of chickens who got in the way, and began closing the gap between us.

Pete darted under the red pickup that was parked there in front of the corrals, and I was just about ready to start tearing off tires and fenders when . . .

Mercy! Was that perfume I smelled?

I lifted my nose, which was somewhat scarred and bleeding, and tested the wind. Yes, perfume. What we had here was The Case of the Strange Perfume, and it would have been the height of irresponsibility for me to continue chasing the cat when I had this new case under way.

I left Pete and followed the scent over to the next pickup, the brown one. Or was it green? One or the other, brown or green. I slipped past the front and peeked around the fender. There sat . . . Drover? How could that be? Drover didn't wear perfume. The pieces of the puzzle just didn't fall into place—until I remembered that Drover had disobeyed my orders and had come down to talk with . . . ah yes, now it was coming back.

The lovely Miss Scamper!

Drover grinned and wagged his stump tail. "Hi Hank. You've got some red flies on your nose."

I lumbered over to him and gave him a scorching glare. "They're not red flies, Drover, they're battle wounds."

"Oh. They looked like . . ."

"And don't try to change the subject. You thought I was tied up, didn't you? You thought you could disobey my orders and get away with it, didn't you? How foolish of you to think that. I suppose it never occurred to you that I might break this rope and walk away a free dog."

"That never occurred to me."

"That's too bad, Drover, because something else is fixing to occur to you."

"Uh-oh."

"That's correct. You're under arrest for insubordination. Go to your room."

"I don't have a room."

"Go somewhere. In other words, buzz off. I have some questions to ask . . ." She was looking down at me, her long beagle ears waving in the breeze, her big brown eyes full of adoration. And I, being a gentleman, said, "Hello again."

"Well, hello there, you big hairy thing dragging a rope around."

"You like that rope? I broke it just for you, just so I could come down here and feast my eyes on the roast beef of your face."

"You have a way with words. The only question is—which way?"

She laughed. I laughed. We both laughed, sharing that special secret shared by two people who laugh at secrets. I could tell she was impressed.

"That's some nose you have there," she went on.

"Battle wounds, Miss Scamper, nothing to worry about. Would you believe me if I told you that you are the most stuntingly beautiful woman I ever saw?"

She arched one brow. "Well now, I don't believe everything I hear, but you might be able to talk me into that."

"Tell me what I can do to make you believe it."

Drover barged into the conversation. "Hank, there's cattle coming this way."

"Hush, Drover. Tell me, Miss Scamper, what can I do to convince you that my heart is in the right place?"

"Take it out and let me look at it."

"I beg your pardon?"

"Don't believe everything I say, big boy. It could get you into trouble."

"Oh, I see. You were joking? Ha ha, ho ho. 'Take

it out and let me look at it.' Yes, I can see how that could get a guy into trouble, taking out his heart and letting . . . you have a strange and delightful sense of humor, Miss Scamper."

"And it was subtle too, until you came along."

"Exactly. I don't know how you've managed all these years without me."

"It's been a real struggle."

"I can imagine! It might surprise you to know that I'm quite a humorist myself, Miss Scamper."

"You hide it very well."

"Hank," that was Drover again, "cattle are coming in."

"Will you please shut your little trap? Thank you." Back to the lovely lady. "Yes, I've always tried to disguise my humor behind a gruff facade, a French word meaning 'the front part of anything.'"

Her eyes widened in amazement. "I didn't know you spoke French too."

"Oh yes. French, Thousand Island, Open-gloppish, Pig Latin, Spanish, as well as several of the coyalect diotes . . . coyote dialects, that is."

"My goodness, you've been a busy boy!"

"Indeed I have. In the Security Business . . ."

Drover was beginning to hop up and down.

"Hank, something's going on, the cattle are coming this way, and here comes that new cowdog."

I peered out into the pasture. Sure enough, Benny the So-called Cowdog was padding toward us. "You're right, Drover, and if I were a betting dog, I would bet that we're fixing to have a show-down."

Miss Scamper's eyes sparkled. "Not over me, I hope."

"I'm afraid so, ma'am. You and several other matters."

"Oooo, this is too exciting!"

"You haven't seen anything yet, Miss Scamper."

"I know, but I can hardly wait."

"This thing could get real nasty before it gets dirty. Stand back, Drover, I wouldn't want you to get hurt."

"Me too." He took cover behind my highly conditioned body—not a bad place to hide.

The imposter came up to the pickups. I squared my shoulders and waited. Some ten feet away, he stopped and glanced around. Perhaps he thought I didn't notice that he winked at Miss Scamper, and perhaps she thought I didn't notice that she winked back, but as you may have already surmised, I did.

"And so, Benny, we meet again," I said in one of my smoother tones of voice. "I'm not sure this ranch is both enough for big of us."

"Do you suppose you fellows could move out of the way?" he said. "We're trying to bring in cattle." His eyes fell upon me. "Are those red flies on your nose, sport?"

"No, as I've explained to everyone else on this ranch, those are battle wounds."

"Yes, I see that now. But aren't you supposed to be tied?"

"Yes, I was tied. Yes, I broke the rope. No, we're not moving out of the way. And no, you're not bringing in any cattle without my permission. Any more questions?"

"Just one. Are you completely out of your mind?" At that very moment, and for reasons which I didn't understand, Miss Scamper nodded her head. "Because this is a roundup, you see, and we have work to do and you really don't fit into the overall dynamics."

"That's where you're wrong, Benny. I've let this thing go far enough, and now I'm fixing to shut 'er down. The fact of the matter is that YOU don't fit into the overall hydraulics."

"Uh *dynamics,* I think is the word you wanted."

"I said what I meant, Benny, and I'm afraid the old trick of putting words into my mouth won't work this time."

He gave his head a quick shake. "Good heavens, I thought I'd seen it all."

"No, as a matter of fact, you've only seen the beginning. Now pack your bags and get off my ranch."

He gave me a smirk. "You obviously don't understand what you're saying, so I'll not argue. We WILL bring in the cattle, your opinions on the matter notwithstanding."

I took two steps toward him. "Benny, old buddy, let me tell you something. I'll be withstanding in the gate when you start those cattle this way, and I'll see to it that you're exposed for what you are—an imposter and a fraud."

He glanced up at Miss Scamper. "Is he joking, do you suppose?"

"I don't know, but I thought you boys were going to fight."

I took another step toward Benny the Imposter. "That's correct, Miss Scamper. The fight will start very soon. This is a showdown, Benny, me against you."

Benny smiled. "You understand, of course, that the cowboys are involved in this too. It goes beyond whatever personal animosities we may have."

"Yes, I understand that I'll be outnumbered six to one. I understand that the odds are against me, but I didn't get to be Head of Ranch Security by playing it safe."

"I suppose not. Well, it appears there's nothing more to be said."

"Exactly. Bring on the cattle and we'll see who's the cowdog around here."

He shrugged and then bowed toward Miss Scamper. "I hope this doesn't cause you any inconvenience, madame."

She fluffed at her hair. "I'll manage somehow. I've always loved rassling." Benny left and went back to the herd. She watched him and I watched her.

"Don't waste your time with that guy, Miss Scamper. If you could buy him for what he's worth and sell him for what he thinks he's worth, you'd be a wealthy woman."

"I could go for that."

"Now, if you'll excuse me, I must prepare for combat."

"Oooo! It sounds very dangerous."

"Yes ma'am, but all in a day's work. Just keep your eyes on me and enjoy the show. Come on, Drover, let's . . ." Hmm, that was odd. Drover had been standing right behind . . .

I was in the process of wondering what that might mean when I heard the thunder of hooves moving in my direction. That could mean only one thing: the cattle were coming and my test was about to begin.

Fine. I was ready.

CHAPTER EIGHT

The Big Showdown

Dragging the rope behind me, I took up my position in the middle of the open gate. Nothing would pass through that gate without my permission. And since I had no intention of giving my permission, it followed, through simple logic, that nothing would pass through the gate.

As I waited for the lines of battle to take shape, I heard a familiar voice, the insolent whine of a certain cat. He had ventured out from under the pickup and was licking himself beside the right front tire.

"Hi Hankie. You never did catch me, did you?"

"There's a reason for that, kitty. I lost interest in your particular brand of foolishness and had more important things to do than chase a rinky-dink cat around the ranch. As a matter of fact, I have more important things to do than *talk* to a rinky-dink cat."

"Well, you should just quit talking."

"I will, I did, I am. That's what I just said."

"But you're still talking."

"Of course I am, for the simple reason that it's not possible for me to tell you that I'm not talking to you without telling you."

He looked up and smiled. "But you're still talking."

"No, quite the contrary. I've made it very plain that I'm breaking off all communication with you."

"But you keep talking about it, Hankie."

I pushed myself up on all-fours and swaggered over to him. "Are you trying to get me into an argument?"

"Certainly not."

"Yes you are."

"No I'm not."

"Yes you are, yes you are, yes you are! But I want you to know, cat, that I'm not so easily fooled."

"Yes you are."

"No I'm not. I will not, cannot, and shall not be lured into an argument with a sniveling, insignificant, insolent, two-bit, rinky-dink cat. Because I have better things to do."

"No you do."

"Yes I don't."

"No you do."

"Yes I don't! I don't have anything better to do than . . ." I had somehow lost the thread of the argument, although we weren't actually arguing because I had . . . "I have said my last word on the subject."

"You have?"

"Yes."

"Oops, there's another one."

"That wasn't a word."

"No it wasn't."

"Yes it was."

"No, it was not a word."

"YES IT WAS A WORD!"

"I don't want to argue about it, Hankie."

"Well, that's too bad, because when you try to play with the big boys, you'd better be prepared to defend yourself."

"May I ask you a question, Hankie?"

"No."

"Good, because I'm not going to talk to you anymore."

I gave him a growl. "Ask the question, cat, and be quick about it."

"Promise not to argue?"

"I promise nothing to the likes of you. I'll argue any time I choose. Now ask the question."

He licked his paw. "What were you doing in the middle of the gate?"

"That's simple, cat. I was ... HUH?"

I glanced to my left and saw that cattle were, so to speak, passing through the gate. Suddenly, all the clues began ...

I turned back to Pete, and this time I was ready to sweep the ranch with his mangy carcass, but he was sitting under the pickup, grinning at me and flicking his tail back and forth.

"Let that be a lesson to you, cat!" I yelled, and rushed back to my combat position.

Even though I was stepped on three times and horned once, I fought my way through the stream of moronic cows, seized control of the gate, set up a strong defensive position, and began barking.

A small number of animals, perhaps eight or ten, had slipped through my lines before I got there, but that was a small price to pay for my triumph over the cat. Yes, Benny the Imposter had scored a few points on me, but it was still early in the game.

I barked. I snapped. I snarled. I gave them old sookies the full nine yards of defensive strategy. In a matter of seconds, I had them milling in front of the gate, and one minute into the maneuver, they turned south and broke into a wild stampede.

Oh, success! Oh, triumph! Oh, happy day! Single-handledly, with nothing but guts and brains and brute strength, I had foiled Benny the Imposter's plot, saved the ranch, and rescued my reputation from the edge of the brink.

And best of all, Miss Scamper had watched the entire battle from her box seat in the pickup bed. I would have died a thousand deaths to see that sparkle in her eyes, but, fortunately, that wasn't necessary.

Well, I had cleaned up another mess and was about to go strutting over to bask in Miss Scamper's adoring gaze, when I noticed a lone horseman riding my way—perhaps to congratulate me on my triumph over Benny the Imposter?

It was High Loper. He was riding hard. He was swinging his rope. He was yelling naughty words. He appeared to be . . .

In this line of work, it's virtually impossible to please everyone all the time. Sometimes, in the course of accomplishing one objective, a guy runs afoul of other objectives, and this appeared to be . . .

Okay. Let's get it over with. Loper was mad, furious, and I had reason to suspect that his anger was directed at . . . well, me. I began to suspect this when he came thundering toward me, shouting evil things and swinging his rope.

"YOU IDIOT DOG, GIT OUT OF THAT GATE!"

I have said many times that Hank the Cowdog can take a hint. That's the truth. It's been true for years and it remains true to this very day. Okay. I wasn't wanted there in the gate? Fine. I would just leave.

I left, taking the shortest distance between two points, which happened to be right between the legs of the colt. Had I remembered that I was dragging a ten-foot rope, I might have chosen a different route, for even though Loper had threatened my life and shouted wicked things about me, I had no wish to frighten his colt and get him . . .

It's a well known fact in ranch circles that many green colts are afraid of ropes, especially ropes dragged between their . . .

It's a rare colt indeed that will stand still for such a thing, and this particular colt, whose name was Jughead, did not even come close to standing still.

I happened to be looking back over my shoulder and saw the entire incident. All four of Jughead's legs went out in different directions and his neck somehow wrapped around the underside of his chest, so that I caught a glimpse of his moon-shaped eyes, looking back at me through the corridor of his legs.

An instant later, his back end shot skyward, and poor Loper, who was still shaking his fist at me, went along with it.

The colt's rear end came back down but Loper didn't. He flew out of his stirrups, arched over the saddle lot gate, and entered the saddle shed without opening the door, so to speak.

It wasn't a heavy door or very fancy, made of three-eights plywood, as I recall, and he went right through it, made quite a crash.

Well, naturally I was concerned. I mean, Loper and I have had our differences through the years, but still, we worked for the same outfit and certain bonds . . . so I stopped to see how badly he was hurt.

I thought about rushing to his side and licking his face. Sometimes that helps, you know.

He picked himself up off the floor and staggered to the door and looked out. His hat was on crooked. He saw me and leveled a finger at me. And here's what he said to his loyal friend and companion, the dog who had stopped to check on his condition:

"Where's my gun? Bring me a gun! IF I HAD A GUN . . ."

Well, that was enough for me. I wasn't foolish enough to suppose that he wanted to go quail hunting at that time of the morning, so I turned south and headed for the timber along the creek.

Seemed to me this might be a good time to vanish for a while. Little did I know what trouble lay in store for me.

CHAPTER NINE

Found by
the Coyote
Brotherhood

I had done such an excellent job of turning the cattle away from the gate that they had not only left the gate, they had pretty muchly left the country.

I could see them in two's and three's, running toward the north side of the pasture, with cowboys whipping and spurring in pursuit.

Actually, I hadn't planned to throw such a scare into them. Scoring a few points against Benny the Imposter was one thing, but wrecking the entire roundup . . .

One of the dangers of being as big and ferocious as I am is that it's hard to make a *small* impression. Everyone takes you seriously, don't you see, and the next thing you know, the small impression you intended to make becomes larger than life, so to speak.

And, as I've indicated, this seemed a good time to lay low for a while. I headed down to the creek and vanished in the heavy undergrowth of willows that grew along its sandy banks.

This was an excellent place to hide out, since the willows were virtually imponderable . . . implausible . . . implacable . . . impeachable, I know there's a word that just fits what I'm trying to say here, it's a big word, begins with "im-" and I get a kick out of using big words once in a while, but it appears that I've lost it for the moment. Imperceptible? No.

Well, never mind. Sometimes big words are more trouble than they're worth and a guy would be better off using simple language.

The willows were so thick that a man on horse-back couldn't ride through them, and now that I've said it, I remember the derned word: im-pen-e-tra-ble. That's a big rascal, no wonder I couldn't spit it out.

Where was I? Oh yes, in the imperceptible willows. Once inside the willows, I vanished without a trace. My plan at this point, to the extent that I had a plan at all, was to stay out of sight and camp out for several days, until my little misunderstanding with Loper blew over and the cowboys were ready to forgive and forget.

Peeking out of the brush, I saw Loper climb back on his colt and ride hard for the east side of the pasture. I could also see Benny the Imposter, trying to turn a couple of cows and calves that were heading for the brush. I didn't wish him any bad luck, but since he seemed to be having it anyway, that was okay with me.

I went down to the creek and got a drink, looked at the handsome face in the water and found myself admiring the nose, the shape of the head, the ears, the stern set of the eyes, the hard curve of mouth which suggested a bold and shrewd mind at work, the hair, the massive shoulders that rippled with muscles and tapered down to feet that could have been used as a pattern for all feet, for while they appeared to be graceful and delicate at first glance, they were in fact the perfect tools of a sprinting machine.

It has been said that all understanding begins with the feet, which just goes to show how important they are.

Anyway, for half an hour or so, I stood by the water's edge, near hypnotized by the reflection I saw. All great works of art don't hang in museums. Sometimes you find them in unlikely places.

I liked everything I saw in the reflection except the rope, which was still tied around my neck.

I had no use for that rope and decided it was time to get shed of it. It occurred to me that by lowering my jaw and moving my head backward on its pivotal spinal whatever-you-may-call-it, I could get the rope into my mouth and then make hash of it with my long sharp teeth.

I tried this for quite a while without what you would call great success. I discovered: A) that it is virtually impossible to get a good biting position on a rope around one's neck; and B) if one moves one's head backward far enough, what often happens is that one topples over backward.

So there you are. Sometimes it's easier to accept life's imperfections than to chew them in half.

Having finished my business at the water's edge, I became bored and decided to move on down the creek to look for new adventure and fresh scenery, yet I had not planned to find the type of adventure and scenery upon which I stumbled upon.

As I was passing through the jungle, the end of my ten-foot piece of rope lodged itself in the fork of a willow. I tried to uproot the tree but found this near-impossible—or, to express it another way, *impossible*.

Most trees do not uproot well.

Denied this solution to my problem, I abandoned the solution, yet the problem remained. What to do? That was the question. I was in the process of studying it from many different angles when, suddenly, I heard footsteps approaching through the jungle.

Since I couldn't think of anyone I wanted to meet at that particular moment, I flattened myself out on the ground and tried to blend in with the surrounding fauna and fluoride.

The footsteps came closer, and then they stopped—very near to the spot where I lay, invisible to naked eyes. And speaking of eyes, I rolled mine around in their sprockets until I could see two heads suspended above me.

Further inspection revealed that the heads were attached to necks, the necks to bodies, and the bodies to legs and so forth. Upon seeing the sharp-pointed noses and yellow eyes of the suspects, I said to myself, "I think I've seen these guys before somewhere." And no sooner had that thought skipped across my mind than one of the suspects spoke.

"Uh! We find Hunk Dog lying in jungle, far away from house and boom-boom!"

Perhaps I should intrude here to give a translation, for you see, the suspects in this case turned out to be none other than the notorious coyote brothers, Rip and Snort.

Little wonder that I felt I had seen them before, because I had seen them before—not once or twice or thrice or frice, but many times, and always under awkward conditions.

For you see, any time a guy runs into a pair of cannibals, the conditions are likely to be awkward. These guys were terrible!

Coyotes, you might recall, speak a peculiar dialect. Any dog who goes into full-time security work should be fluent in several languages, including the coyote dialect. At the risk of tooting my own horn, I should point out that I am something of a whiz at languages, always have been, even the ancient and primitive dialect of the *Coyotus Cannibalus*.

With that out of the way, let us proceed to the translation and take another look at the statement under our microscope, so to speak: "Uh! We find Hunk Dog lying in jungle, far away from house and boom-boom!"

The first word uttered by this savage, you will notice, was the one syllable exclamation, "Uh!" This is one of the most commonly used words in the coyote dialect. Our studies of the talkatory patterns of wild coyotes indicate that coyotes are partial to short words.

"Uh" is just about as short as a word can be. Any coyote who shortened it further would find himself saying either "U" or "h," neither of which makes much sense, even to coyotes.

Why do coyotes prefer short words? Good question.

My own personal theory is that short words such as "Uh" are hard to misspell and mispronounce, and are therefore popular with these miserable, lice-bitten creatures of the prairie.

You'll notice that Snort referred to me as "Hunk" instead of the usual "Hank," and perhaps you wondered why. Here, we have a choice of explanations:

1) "Hunk" is the coyote word for "Hank."
2) For unknown reasons, coyotes are not able to pronounce "Hank."
3) Snort was not too bright and didn't even know that he was butchering my name.

That should cover the "Hunk" part of the mystery. Now, let's hurry on to the last two words in the translation: "boom-boom" and "house."

As I have pointed out before, "boom-boom" is

the coyote word for "gun." We have found evidence suggesting that "boom-boom" has some relationship to the sound made by a gun. When fired, a weapon does not make the sound, "gun-gun," so . . . I think you get the point.

This process of creating a word from an actual sound is called "onomatopetunia." Just thought I'd throw that in.

And that brings us to the coyote word, "house." As odd as it might seem, "house" in coyote language means "house." That does seem odd, doesn't it? But there you are.

Well, with all the technical stuff out of the way, we can proceed to the chilling, spine-tingling adventures that resulted from my chance meeting with these two bloodthirsty cannibals out in the jungle.

And don't forget: because the end of my rope had snagged on a willow tree, I wasn't able to run away. Not that I would have run away under different conditions, but let us say that I would have considered it a very attractive option.

On the other hand . . . yes, I would have run away. Of course I would have! No dog in his right mind would talk to cannibals in the jungle, for as Snort had shrewdly observed, they had caught me a long way from house and boom-boom.

CHAPTER TEN

The Wolf Creek Decathalon

Since they had caught me red-handed in broad daylight, I figgered there was no future in trying to pretend I wasn't there.

I raised my head and tried to put on a pleasant face. "Good morning, fellers. Before we get involved in other matters, let me say a few words..."

Snort held up one paw. "Hunk not talk crazy stuff like last time."

"Who me? Well, I don't know what you're..."

"Rip and Snort not like fooled all time."

"Yes, I see what you..."

"Rip and Snort tired and hungry, all night singing and carrying on, not have time to hunt. Maybe we eat dog."

I swallowed. "Uh... dog?" Snort nodded. Rip

licked his chops. Already we were off to a bad start. "How about a cat? I know where you can find a nice, fat, juicy cat."

"Dog quick and easy meal. And dog tied up too, not hard catch, ho ho."

"Yes . . . ho, ho. You're referring to the rope, I suppose." They nodded. "And my being tied up, so to speak." They nodded. "That is, you probably think I'm tied up and can't run and play and so forth." They nodded. "It does appear that way, doesn't it?" They nodded. "Would you guys care to hear the true story about this rope?"

"Only true story. Not want more crazy stuff, like moon made of chopped chicken liver."

I forced a chuckle. "Oh, that one. Yes, I remember the night I told you guys that story, and I admit that it was a little . . . uh . . . that is, it contained elements of fiction, as well as . . ."

"Big lie. Made Rip and Snort look stupid."

"Stupid? Surely not. I mean, I wouldn't have . . ."

Snort put his sharp nose right down in my face. "Hunk waste time. Talk quick. Then we eat."

"Eat? Who could eat at a time like this? I mean, it's too late for breakfast and too early for supper, and then there's always the chance that after hearing my story, you'll decide, completely on your own and with no prompting from me . . ."

He showed me his teeth and growled.

". . . on second thought, maybe I should go right into my story, you suppose?"

"Uh."

"All right, here we go. Are you ready for this?" No answer, just unblinking yellow stares. "All right. Now, at first glance, it appears that I'm tied to that tree stump, right?" No response, nothing. "But first impressions are often misleading, I'm sure you've noticed that, haven't you, of course you have."

Blank stares. I went on.

"But here's the straight story, guys. Not more than an hour ago, one of the cowboys noticed that this part of the pasture was starting to move— and I mean drift, shift, float away. You can imagine what a disaster that could be if part of the pasture just by George picked up and moved away."

Rip scratched a flea on his ear. It was hard to tell if I was getting through to them.

"We can come back to that later if you have any questions, or we could pause here and . . ." Snort shook his head. "No, let's move along. Well, Slim was worried about what might happen if the pasture moved away. I mean, let's face it, nobody really knows what's under this pasture, and so he brought me down here—I'm the Head of Ranch Security, you see, and in emergency situations . . ."

Snort poked me in the chest with his paw. "Get to point of story, not mess around with bunch talk."

"I'm getting there. In fact, I'm there already. Here's the point. Slim brought me down here for one purpose and one purpose only: to hold down this section of the pasture and keep it from drifting away."

"Uh."

"That explains why the stump is tied to me. And I'm sure you've already figgered out what might happen if I were suddenly, well, eaten."

"Uh."

"But just in case you haven't, let me explain. In a matter of minutes, this entire section of the pasture could drift away, leaving a bottomless pit in its place—and I'm talking about a deep, black bottomless pit with no bottom. I'll bet that scares you, huh?"

They shook their heads. "Not scared because Rip and Snort not believe one word of lying stupid story."

"Not even one little word?"

They pushed up off their haunches and came

a step closer. Their glittering eyes made me uneasy. "Now time for eat and then take big nap."

It was time for me to make a break for freedom. I hit the end of the rope with a full head of steam, hoping that it would break one more time, only it didn't and I did a back flip and landed hard on the ground.

I coughed and staggered to my feet. "All right, you've got me cornered. I'll admit that. But aren't you forgetting something? What about the ancient coyote custom of letting a captive fight for his life?"

Big smiles spread across their faces. "Uh! Fight? Coyote never too busy for big fight."

"Exactly. But instead of engaging in your ordinary tooth-and-toenail kind of brawl, I challenge you both to a series of contests that will test our skill and courage."

"Uh!"

"If I win, I'm a free dog. If I lose, I'm a free lunch. What do you say? Do you have guts enough to put your lousy reputations on the line?"

"Coyote have plenty guts and not scared for lousy reputation. Hunk not have chance."

"Maybe so, Snort, but you've got it to do. All right, here's the first event: the rope-chewing contest. The first one to chew this rope in two is the winner. Ready?" They knocked each other down taking their positions at the rope. "On your mark. Get set. Go!"

It's amazing what a stinking, illiterate coyote can do to a piece of stout rope. Those guys took two snaps each and amputated a two-foot section from the bottom end of the rope. I finished dead-last, which was all right, since I didn't care for the oily taste of the rope anyway. Cable, I should say.

Snort spit the cable out of his mouth and gave me a big grin. "Ha ha! Hunk lose pretty big."

"Yes, so it appears. But I think you just got lucky."

"Uh? Not luck. Win because berry tough."

"Well, we'll see about that. This next event will be a real test of your . . ."

At that moment, I heard a flutter of wings and the sound of branches snapping in the cottonwood tree above us. Rip and Snort heard it too. We all looked up and saw . . . not cattle, as you might have suspected, but two big black ugly birds sitting on a limb some ten feet above us.

I recognized them at once: Wallace and Junior, the buzzards. And I can't say that I was glad to see them. When buzzards arrive on the scene, it usually means that somebody's luck has gone sour.

My luck was getting better, but it still wasn't out of the woods, so to speak. Yes, I had tricked

the coyotes into chewing my rope in two, but I didn't dare make a break for freedom. Not yet, not while those thugs were still in good running condition.

Wallace stuck out his skinny neck and looked us over. "Y'all go ahead on, don't pay any attention to us. We come early to make some side bets, is all we done, and then we're gonna stay for dinner."

"Oh yeah?" I yelled. "Who says there's going to BE any dinner? As a matter of fact, we're in the midst of the First Annual Wolf Creek Decathalon, and although it might appear that the coyotes have a small lead at this point . . ."

"The coyotes have a BIG lead, pup, we seen it all from the air, and Junior, I'm taking the coyotes and giving three-to-one odds."

"Uh-uh okay, P-P-Pa, and I'll t-t-take my d-d-doggie friend, doggie friend."

Wallace gave his head a shake. "Son, don't ever bet on your friends or your kinfolks. It causes hard feelings when you go to eat, so just play the odds and never mind the friendship. I've told you that before."

"Y-yeah, I g-g-guess s-so."

"Because, son, the world's divided into three parts: heart, mind, and stomach."

"Y-y-yeah."

"And you should always listen to that still, small voice in your stomach. It'll never lie to you or let you down. No buzzard has ever got a broken heart by listening to his stomach."

"Y-y-yeah, but he's s-s-still my f-f-friend and my p-p-pal, and we s-s-s-sing together, sing together."

"He AIN'T your friend and he AIN'T your pal and he can't sing any better than I can, and I can't sing at all, but you ARE gonna bet on him because I've got the coyotes at three-to-one."

"Uh . . . okay."

"And I've told you over and over and over, you cut out this silly talk about bein' a singer when you grow up, nobody in my family has ever been a singer and nobody in my family is ever gonna be a singer, and when my coyote boys win, I get first dibs on a hind laig."

I guess Snort didn't like that. He looked up into the tree and curled his lip. "Buzzard get big hurt, not first dibs."

"Well, we'll just see about that, and in the meantime, y'all hurry up, we ain't had a bite to eat in three days, this boy of mine is old enough to be taking care of his poor old daddy but he's such a ninny, hurry up, would you please?"

Rip and Snort grinned and shook their heads.

"Coyote not take orders from buzzard. Coyote do what coyote want, ho ho."

Old man Wallace leaned down and stuck out his tongue. "Well ho-ho your own self, and DON'T hurry up, see if I care, 'cause we got no place else to go and nuthin' else to do."

"Uh!" Snort turned back to me and poked me in the chest. "That better. Hurry up."

I had kind of hoped the argument would drag on for a couple of days. Give Hank the Cowdog two or three days and he'll always find a way to get out of a jam. But it appeared that my time frame had been shortened to something like fifteen minutes.

This was my last chance, fellers. I was fixing to walk a tightrope across the canyon of life, and from here on, the story gets pretty scary.

CHAPTER ELEVEN

Out-Singing
the Cannibals

I took a deep breath and tried to calm my nerves. Ordinarily, my nerves resemble high-grade steel, but competing in front of cannibals and buzzards has always bothered me.

"All right," I said to my opponents, "you guys won the first round." They nodded. "Through sheer luck, if you ask me." They shook their heads. "But luck won't save you in this next event. It's going to be a test of brute skill."

"Coyote not scared. Got plenty brute and plenty skill."

"We'll see about that. This next event will be a contest to see which of us can sing the better song."

The brothers broke out laughing. "Ha ha!

Hunk lose for sure this time. Rip and Snort sing better than whole world!"

"Maybe and maybe not. I happen to have a real crackerjack of a song myself. You guys go first."

Snort shook his head. "Hunk not give orders. Hunk go first."

"All right, if that's the way you want it, you guys go second."

Snort showed his fangs. "Hunk not give orders! Hunk go second!"

"All right, but I'll have to file a protest over this. I wanted the first shot."

"Uh. Coyote always take first shot."

The brothers went into a huddle and planned their song. While they were whispering their signals, Wallace grumbled about how he wished they would hurry up. At last, the brothers turned around.

I had expected them to sing "Me Just a Worthless Coyote," the Coyote Sacred Hymn and National Anthem. I'd heard that one before, and in fact, I'd helped them sing it on a few occasions. I knew my song would beat it.

To be real honest about it, I didn't suppose, they knew another song. But they did. This one was entirely new. It was called, "Daddy Packed His Suitcase 'Cause Momma Was a Mean Old Bag." In the middle of it, Rip pulled out a trombone and played a solo, kind of surprised me, I didn't know he had that kind of talent. Here's how it went.

Daddy Packed His Suitcase 'Cause Momma Was a Mean Old Bag

Daddy had a weakness for wimmen who could
    spit and cuss.
He liked 'em mean and ragged because he
    didn't care to discuss
The finer points of love and eternal bliss,
He had no use for tenderness.
Oh, Daddy was a villain looking for a villainess.

Well, he met our ma at a waterhole, they said
    that she was having a drink,
She was sitting in a corner and said she didn't
    think
There was a man in the world who could
    tame her down,
She could whup any man in Coyote Town.
Daddy said he wanted a wildcat, and fellers,
    that's what he'd found.

He walked up to our momma and slapped her
    right across the chops.

She kicked him in the brisket and slugged
    him with a wicked right cross.
He knocked her to the floor but she jumped
    right up,
Loosened five front teeth and yelled,
    "Beware, old pup!"
Oh, Daddy screamed and hollered,
He'd found himself the girl of his dreams.

They were married in a junkyard, the honey-
    moon was spent in a fight.
This was coyote love for certain.
Instead of trading kisses, they'd bite.
Daddy stayed around until he lost a bout
And then he hit the road 'cause Momma
    threw him out.
Oh, Daddy packed his suitcase 'cause
    Momma was a mean old,
A not so very clean old,
Our momma was a mean old bag.

When Rip and Snort finished, they whooped
and hollered and slapped each other on the back.
They were real tickled with their performance,
and I had to admit it was impressive.

"Ha! Hunk not have chance against coyote love
song!"

"Is that what it was? I guess love gets pretty rough in your neighborhood."

"Everything rough in coyote neighborhood. Coyote like tough old gals."

"I see what you mean."

Up in the tree, old man Wallace had to put in his two cents worth. "Now Junior, that's what I call *music*. I don't know why you can't sing good wholesome country-western instead of that noisy stuff you do with that dog. And yes, I think we have a winner. My coyote boys have definitely won the contest."

"Hold on, buzzard," I called out. "You haven't heard my song yet."

"No, but I've heard you before, puppy, and I know real talent when I don't hear it and anyways, I'm bettin' on the other side, and if you ask me . . ."

"I don't think anybody asked you, and I have my doubts that anybody ever will. When it comes to music and culture, the opinions of a buzzard don't carry much weight around here."

"'Well, that just tells you what kind of cheapjohn outfit you're runnin' here, and just for that, I'm gonna sleep through your whole song."

I gave him a dark and angry look, but the truth of the matter was that I couldn't have been more pleased. Wallace didn't know it, but he was walking right into my trap.

I turned back to the coyote brothers. They were staring at me with stupid grins and heavy eyes. They had been up all night and had mentioned that they were tired, right? I couldn't expect a fair deal in a singing contest with a couple of cannibals, right? And they planned to eat me immediately after my performance, right?

Hencely, my only hope of escape lay in putting the whole bunch to sleep, and it happened that I had chosen a song that just might do it.

"Are you guys ready for this?"

"Ready for Hunk lose contest." Snort chuckled and then broke into a big, toothy yawn.

"Hold on. I don't want you guys going to sleep on me. I stayed awake through that dreary thing of yours, and you have to stay awake and listen to mine."

The grin vanished from Snort's mouth. "Hunk not give orders to coyote. Coyote not take orders from lunch meat."

"All right, but I don't want you going to sleep in the middle of my song."

"Coyote sleep when coyote want sleep, never mind what Hunk think. Sing!"

"Very well, Snort, if that's the way you want to be. Here goes. Junior, why don't you help me on the chorus? I'd like to spiffy it up a little bit, and with your gorgeous voice and my gorgeous voice . . ."

Junior grinned and nodded his head. "Oh bb-boy, that would b-be so m-m-much f-f-f-f-fun!

"All right, here we go."

I turned to the coyote brothers and began my song—or, to put it another way, my secret weapon for putting them to sleep. If it worked, I would live to see another day and solve another mystery. If it didn't . . . I would become coyote fodder.

Hank's Lullaby

Your eyelids are heavy, your eyeballs are
    aching,
Your tongue is fatigued and your four legs
    are shaking and quaking.
Your eardrums are ringing, your nostrils are
    stinging,
It seems to me you should be going to bed.

Sleep, baby, sleep.
Surrender yourself to the call of the deep,
    baby.
Sleep, baby, sleep.
Close your eyes and start counting sheep.

The notion of eating or feasting or feeding
At this time of day when the whole body's
    pleading and bleeding
For sleep is repulsive, remote, and
    convulsive.
You really should think about going to bed!

Sleep, baby, sleep.
Surrender yourself to the call of the deep,
    baby.
Sleep, baby, sleep.
Close your eyes and start counting sheep.

A couple of big handsome guys like yourself
Should stop eating so much and consider
    your health and your waistline
And dog meat, I've read, has more calories
    than bread.
It's a whole lot more fattening than going
    to bed.

Sleep, baby, sleep.
Surrender yourself to the call of the deep,
    baby,
Sleep, baby, sleep.
Close your eyes and start counting sheep.

One two three four five sheep
One two three four five sheep
One two three four five sheep
One two three, one two three four five sheep
One two three four five sheep
One two three four five sheep
One two three four five, a whole bunch of
    sheep

Sleep, baby, sleep.
Surrender yourself to the call of the deep,
    baby,
Sleep, baby, sleep.
Close your eyes and start counting sheep.

CHAPTER TWELVE

I Win the Singing Contest and Rescue the Boss

It worked!

By the time we finished up the last chorus Rip and Snort lay in a big twitching pile on the sand, not merely asleep but out of this world.

And up in the tree, old man Wallace was in the same condition. At any moment, I expected to see him fall off his perch.

"Well, Junior, I'd say we just by George knocked 'em out with our song."

"Y-yeah, something h-h-happened, 'cause they s-s-sure went to s-s-s-s-sleep, went to sleep."

"Just what I wanted them to do, Junior. And now, if you'll excuse me, I'll just ooze out of here and vanish in the underbrush. When your old man wakes up, tell him I'm sorry I couldn't stay for dinner."

"H-he's g-g-gonna be m-m-mad."

"Yes indeed. And you can tell him that he might as well get used to being mad, because any time he deals with Hank the Cowdog, he's going to finish in last place."

I d-d-don't think I'll t-t-t-tell him th-th-that."

"Whatever. See you around, Junior, and thanks for your help on the song."

He gave me a sad smile and waved his wing. "B-b-bye, D-d-d-doggie."

With the stealth of a tiger, I slipped into the jungle and disappeared. While the coyote brothers were asleep, I had to put some mileage between us. They wouldn't sleep forever, you see, and when they awoke, they just might try to follow my scent—also the trace in the sand, left by the rope I was dragging. Cable, I mean.

I picked my way through the willows, heading in a northerly direction, until I came to the edge of the brush. I poked my head out and took a look around the pasture.

I had this problem, you see. Although I had escaped from the cannibals, I couldn't assume that the cowboys would welcome me back with open

arms, so to speak. If you recall, I had been impli-
cated in a stampede, and on our outfit, the cowboys got pretty serious about stampedes.

The long and short of it was that I was
trapped between two hostile forces. I had no good
place to go, and yet going no place would get me
nowhere—if you can follow that.

I headed east, staying out in open country but
close enough to the brush so that I could take
cover if some wild, crazed cowboy came after me
with a loaded rope.

I rounded a bend in the creek, right there by
those big bluffs near the crossing, when all at
once I found myself looking into the face of Benny
the Imposter.

He glared at me and I glared right back. He
spoke first. "You made quite a mess of my roundup, I hope you know."

"It couldn't have happened to a nicer guy."

"Yes, well, I'm trying to clean up your mess,
and if you'll just run along . . ."

"As a matter of fact, if you approached me just
right, I might consider helping you out."

He smirked. "Oh? That's very kind of you,
of course, but I've seen your work and, quite
frankly, I'm not sure you know what you're
doing. I noticed a pattern of non-discipline and

even non-thinking, and that bothers me."

"Oh yeah? Well, I've seen a few patterns my-self, and the one that bothers me most is that you're still on my ranch."

"I understand how hard it must be to go from being top dog to bottom dog, all in one morning."

"I wouldn't know about that. It's never hap-pened to me."

He arched his brows. "Really? I'm sorry, sport, but I'm afraid you've lost your job to a better dog. Now, I have cattle to gather." He turned and

walked a few steps away. Then he stopped. "Oh, by the way, High Loper's horse went down in quicksand and he's pinned. You might want to go help him."

"What? Loper's horse . . ." I felt my temper rising. "Hey, that guy's my master. If you saw that he was in quicksand, why didn't you help him?"

"I am a specialist, highly trained in my discipline. I know nothing and care nothing about rescues. I was brought here to gather cattle, and gather cattle I shall. If doing rescues is something that appeals to you, you're welcome to it. Now, excuse me, I'm already behind schedule."

Before I could jump in the middle of him and give him the whipping he deserved, he disappeared into the jungle. Imagine that! A dog that was too important to help a cowboy in distress! I couldn't believe it.

Well, you might say that High Loper was among the last people I had wanted to see that day, seeing as how he had wanted to shoot me the last time we'd met. But what's a dog to do?

High Loper was my master and, in some ways, my friend. If he was in trouble, I had to help him out.

I went streaking down the creek, over rocks and sand, through brush and cattails. I climbed rivers and swam mountains, barked cattle out of the way, scared three rabbits out of the sagebrush, ran into two tree limbs and bounced off a big stump.

Then, all at once, I saw him up ahead, maybe forty yards upstream from the Parnell watergap. His colt had gone down in a wide pool of water and Loper's right leg was pinned in the stirrup, and—here's the serious part—*the water was up to his chin!*

Well, I was the right dog for this assignment and I knew just what to do. I made a dash to the water's edge and started barking.

"Hank, help! Here, Hank!"

Indeed, my master was in serious trouble, so I took a big breath of air and barked louder than ever.

"The rope, Hank, bring me the rope!"

Rope? What rope? He must have been out of his head, just frightened so badly that he didn't know what he was talking about. So I leaned into my task and switched over to Heavy Barking Mode.

"QUIT BARKING AND BRING ME THAT ROPE!"

I stopped barking and looked around for the . . .

Rope. Rope? ROPE? *R O P E!*

Hey, I had a rope around my neck! By merely jumping into the water and swimming out to him, it was possible that I could . . . good thing I was on my toes, Loper probably wouldn't have noticed . . .

I hit the water with a big kersplash and swam out to him with long, graceful strokes. The colt saw me coming and began to thrash around. Loper's nose went under the water and I thought there for a second that we'd lost him—or at least that I would have to dive down and pull him off the bottom, which I wasn't looking forward to doing.

But then his head came back up. He coughed and sputtered and said, "Come on, Hank, just a few more feet, keep coming, boy!"

I did. I swam right to him, hooked my front paws over his shoulders, and gave him a big, juicy lick on the face, just to let him know that everything was going to be okay.

"Swim for shore, Hank! Go stand on the bank so I can get some leverage on this rope. My foot's mashed against some mud and I think . . ."

The colt started thrashing again and Loper's head went under. I didn't have a second to spare. I shifted into the Very Rapid Dog Paddle Mode and virtually sprinted across the water.

Upon reaching the shore, I didn't even bother to shake myself. I leaned into the rope and pulled. And pulled. And pulled!

At last, I felt his foot release from the mud. I staggered forward and continued to haul him toward the shore. He reached the shallows and stumbled out on the bank. He fell to his hands and knees and gasped for air.

I did a quick turn, rushed over to him, and began licking him again, this time in the ear. By George, we had saved ourselves a cowboy!

He threw his arm around my neck and gave me a squeeze. "Good dog, Hank. For once in your life, you showed up at just the right time."

I didn't know exactly what he meant by that, but I took it as a compliment.

After he had caught his breath, he waded back into the water, caught the colt by the briddle reins, and helped him struggle out of the mud and quicksand. Then, when we were all out on dry land, he cut off the rope around my neck.

"Good thing you broke that rope," he said, patting me on the head, "or I'd have been fish food."

Yes, I'd known that all along. I'd had this strange feeling, you see, a kind of *vision* that something evil was going to happen, and that's why I had . . . your better cowdogs have the ability to predict the future, don't you know, and . . .

Well, by that time the others had gathered the cattle and penned them, and we headed back to the corrals. I marched along beside the horse—well, a little *ahead* of the horse, so that I could clear our path of monsters and enemies, and also to give Miss Scamper a good, clean look at . . . well, ME, you might say.

I mean, there's got to be a payoff somewhere in this life.

As we rode along, Loper looked down at me. "You know, Hank, I was all set to buy that hotshot cowdog for three hundred bucks, but he went past me three times while I was in the quicksand, and he never even barked."

I could have told him that was a sorry dog.

"And I think I'll just save my three hundred bucks . . ."

And maybe buy three hundred dollars' worth of steak and hamburger for old Hank?

". . . and buy myself a new pair of shop-made boots and consider it a heck of a deal. And for you, old pup, it's double dog food."

Hmm. Well, doubles on dog food beats singles. And a kick in the rear.

All the cowboys, all the dogs and cats, everybody on the ranch, everybody in the whole neighborhood turned out to welcome us home. You may not believe this, but somebody had called out a brass band and it was playing marches. Grown men cheered and threw cornfetti and streamers, while little children ran along beside us, throwing flowers and casting adoring glances in my general direction.

I could hear them talking. "There he is! That's Hank the Cowdog."

"You mean, the famous Head of Ranch Security?"

"Yes, and he's even more handsome than I thought."

"Oh, he is handsome! And so courageous and bold!"

Etc, etc.

As I said, I don't expect everyone to believe this report, but I feel it's my duty to record the facts, regardless of the . . . I think you get the point.

Well, once again I had managed to raise triumph out of the rubble of experience. I had saved the ranch, saved the boss, and saved my job. Benny the Imposter had been exposed as a heartless cad, and Miss Scamper was so impressed with my performance that she hardly knew what to say.

When the branding work was done and the cowboys were leaving, she looked down at me with those adoring eyes and tried to express the feelings that were tugging at her heart.

"Well, Miss Scamper, this was just another day in the life of Hank the Cowdog. Any time things get dull down at your place, come back and we'll show you a few more tricks."

"You may be a thorn in the flesh, big boy, but you sure came out of this one smelling like a rose."

I'll always remember the expression on her face as she rode away—the lopsided smile, her eyes rolled back in her head. She was definitely impressed.

When everyone had gone, Drover and I made our way down to the gas tanks and collapsed on our gunnysack beds. I was all set to throw up a long line of Zs.

"Hank, what did Miss Scamper mean when she said that stuff about thorns and roses?"

"Very simple, Drover. She was saying that, even though the world sometimes looks better through rose-colored glasses, it's the thorns that stick to your ribs."

"Oh. That still doesn't make any sense to me."

"In that case, let me add one more comment that should tie it all together and put it in its proper perspective: Good night."

"That's all?"

"That's all, Drover. When the end has ended happily, when the day is done and night has come, there's nothing more to say, except good night and good night."

"Good night, Hank."

"Good night, skonk snort zzzzzzzzzz."

"My name's Drover."

"Skiffer murgle pork chop."

"You going to sleep?"

"Skawwww snort zzzzzzzzzz."

"Oh drat. I'm kind of sleepy myzzzzelf."

"Skiffering murgle zzzzz whicklesnort."

"I guess it's morgle snorgle chickenbone zzzzzzzzzzzzzzz."

"Zzzzzzzzzz muddleskaw snort."
"Miggle sniggle snort zzzzzzzzz."

```
                        Z
                        Z
                        Z
                        Z
                        Z
                        Z
Z Z Z Z Z Z Z Z Z Z Z Z Z Z Z Z Z Z Z Z Z Z Z Z Z
                                            Z Z
Snore                                    Z Z
                                      Z Z
        Wheeze                     Z Z
                                Z Z
            Snort             Z Z
                          Z Z
                       Z Z
                    Z Z
                 Z Z          Snore
              Z Z
            Z Z                      Wheeze
         Z Z
      Z Z                                    Snort
   Z Z
Z Z Z Z Z Z Z Z Z Z Z Z Z Z Z Z Z Z Z Z Z Z Z Z Z
```